RICKY RICOTTA'S MIGHTY ROBOT

VS. THE STUPID STINKBUGS FROM SATURN

STORY BY
DAV PILKEY

ART BY
DAN SANTAT

SCHOLASTIC INC.

FOR QUINLAN AND ORLA KEANE
– D.P.

FOR JILL AND IRA
– D.S.

Text copyright © 2003, 2015 by Dav Pilkey
www.pilkey.com

Illustrations copyright © 2015 by Dan Santat
www.dantat.com

Library of Congress Cataloging-in-Publication Data

Pilkey, Dav, 1966 – author.
Ricky Ricotta's mighty robot vs. the stupid stinkbugs from Saturn /
story by Dav Pilkey ; art by Dan Santat. — Revised edition.
pages cm
Summary: Ricky Ricotta, his Mighty Robot, cousin Lucy, and some friends set out to save mousekind from Stupid Stinkbugs from Saturn, with a little help from some special gum and taffy.
1. Ricotta, Ricky (Fictitious character) — Juvenile fiction. 2. Mice — Juvenile fiction. 3. Robots — Juvenile fiction. 4. Cousins — Juvenile fiction. 5. Heroes — Juvenile fiction. 6. Stinkbugs — Juvenile fiction. 7. Saturn (Planet) — Juvenile fiction. [1. Mice — Fiction. 2. Robots — Fiction. 3. Heroes — Fiction. 4. Humorous stories.] I. Santat, Dan, illustrator. II. Title. III. Title: Ricky Ricotta's mighty robot versus the stupid stinkbugs from Saturn.
PZ7.P63123Rst 2014   813.54 — dc23   2014003715

ISBN 978-0-545-63014-6

12 11 10 9 8 7   17 18 19 20 21/0

Printed in China   38

Revised edition
First printing, March 2015

Book design by Phil Falco

CHAPTERS

CHAPTER ONE
RICKY AND HIS ROBOT

One fine day, Ricky Ricotta and his
Mighty Robot were playing cops and
robbers in their yard.

Ricky liked to play the robber because he was good at hiding.

Ricky's Mighty Robot liked playing the cop because he was good at finding things.

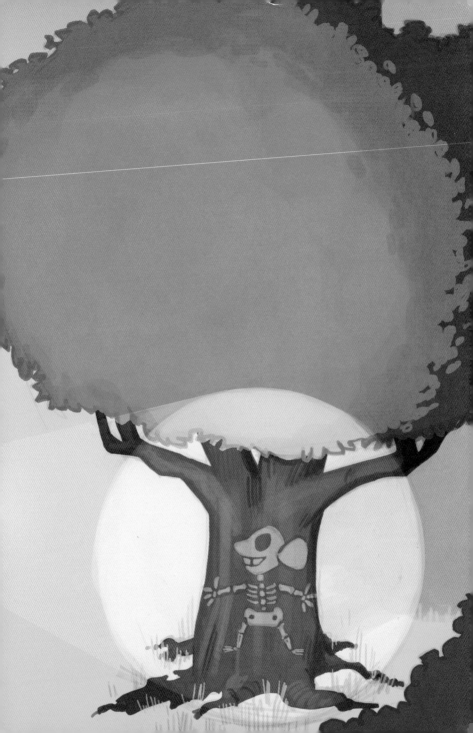

"Hey, no fair," Ricky laughed. "You're not allowed to use X-ray vision!"

Soon Ricky's mother came outside.

"Come along, boys," she said. "We are going to your cousin Lucy's house for lunch."

"Aww, man!" said Ricky. "Do we *have* to go?"

"Yes," said Ricky's mother. "It will be fun."

"But Uncle Freddie always shakes my hand too hard," said Ricky. "And Auntie Ethel always kisses me too much . . . and Cousin Lucy always wants to play *princess!*"

"Well, we are going anyway,"
said Ricky's mother. "So please try
to have some fun."

"We'll go," Ricky sighed, "but
we won't have any fun!"

CHAPTER TWO
UNCLE FREDDIE
AND AUNTIE ETHEL

Soon Ricky and his parents arrived
at Cousin Lucy's house.

"Hello, Ricky, my boy," said
Uncle Freddie. He grabbed Ricky's
hand and shook it hard.

"Ow!" said Ricky.

"Come on, now," said Uncle
Freddie. "Nobody likes a wimpy
handshake!"

Auntie Ethel reached down and kissed Ricky all over his face.

"*Yuck!*" said Ricky.

"Now, now," said Auntie Ethel. "Everybody loves kisses!"

Ricky's Mighty Robot wanted to say hello, too. He reached down and shook Uncle Freddie's hand.

"Owza *yowza!*" shouted Uncle Freddie.

"Nobody likes a wimpy handshake," Ricky giggled.

Then Ricky's Robot gave Auntie
Ethel a big, slobbery kiss.

"What's the matter?" Ricky
laughed. "I thought you *loved* kisses!"

Ricky and his Mighty Robot flew
into the backyard.

There was Lucy, having a tea party
with her pets.

"Wow!" cried Ricky. "Look how big your Jurassic Jackrabbits got!"

"They like to eat," said Lucy. "So I named them Fudgie, Cupcake, and Waffles."

Ricky rolled his eyes.

"Let's play *princess*!" Lucy said.

"No way!" said Ricky.

"Oh, come on," Lucy begged. "I'll be the beautiful princess, and you can be the ugly prince. Fudgie, Cupcake, and Waffles will be our royal ponies, and your Robot can be the big, brave knight."

"What part of *no way* don't you understand?" asked Ricky.

"Now, boys," said Ricky's father, "I want you to play nicely with Lucy."

"Rats!" said Ricky. "This is turning out to be a very bad day."

But what Ricky didn't know was that things were about to get much, much worse.

CHAPTER THREE
SERGEANT STINKBUG

More than 800 million miles away, there was a polluted planet called Saturn, which was overrun with stupid, smelly stinkbugs.

Everywhere you looked, trash filled
the streets . . .

. . . garbage gunked up the rivers . . .

. . . and the factories puffed out so much pollution, it formed a toxic ring of smoke around the whole planet.

But of all the stupid, smelly creatures on Saturn, there was no one stupider or smellier than evil Sergeant Stinkbug. He was the ruler of Saturn, and he was the worst litterbug of all.

Every day when Sergeant Stinkbug
was done eating, he threw his dirty
dishes out the window.

Every night when he was through watching his favorite shows, he tossed his TV out the window.

And every morning when he was
finished sleeping in his bed . . . well,
you get the idea.

Usually, Sergeant Stinkbug loved his smelly, toxic planet. But today, as he strolled through Pollution Parkway, he got fed up.

"This place is a DUMP!" he shouted.

"I want to find a new planet that I can junk up!"

So Sergeant Stinkbug gathered his
stinky subjects, climbed aboard his
Giant Spaceship, and headed for Earth.

CHAPTER FOUR
THE PRINCESS OF EARTH

As the Giant Spaceship approached Earth, Sergeant Stinkbug spoke to his armies.

"Listen up, you stinkers," said the evil Sergeant. "First, we must find the king of Earth and kidnap him. Then, we will take over the planet!"

The Stupid Stinkbugs searched through their Super-Sonic Spy Scope, but they could not find a king. They looked all over Earth, but they couldn't even find a queen.

"Duh, look!" said one of the Stupid Stinkbugs finally. "I think I see a princess!"

The Super-Sonic Spy Scope zoomed in on Lucy, who was standing on the picnic table giving orders.

"You guys have to protect me," Lucy said, "so the bad guys don't steal all of my precious rubies!"

"A-*HA*!" cried Sergeant Stinkbug.
"I'll kidnap that princess and steal all
of those rubies she was talking about.
Then we'll all take over the planet!"

So Sergeant Stinkbug got into his
Attack Pod and headed for Lucy's house.

CHAPTER FIVE
THE PICNIC

Soon it was time for lunch. Ricky's
aunt and uncle brought food out to
everybody. Then they went back
inside to eat with Ricky's parents.

Fudgie, Cupcake, Waffles, Ricky, and his Mighty Robot all dove into their grilled cheese sandwiches.

"C'mon, you guys," Lucy whined. "Let's play *before* we eat."

Suddenly, Sergeant Stinkbug
showed up. He lowered the Automatic
Snatcher Arm on his Attack Pod and
grabbed Lucy.

"Hey, look, everybody," cried Lucy. "A bad guy is trying to steal my rubies!"

"Yeah, *right*," said Ricky, who didn't even bother to turn around.

"C'mon, you guys!" cried Lucy. "Stop eating and save me from this evil space-bug!"

"Boy," said Ricky, "that kid sure has a vivid imagination."

CHAPTER SIX
LUCY IN THE SKY
WITH RUBIES

Sergeant Stinkbug carried Lucy
high into the air and demanded
to know where all the rubies
were.

"They're right here on my
crown, you big dummy!"
said Lucy.

"Those aren't real," said Sergeant Stinkbug. "You just drew those on with crayons!"

"You better put me down before my Jurassic Jackrabbits beat you up!" said Lucy.

"*Ooh!* I'm *so scared!*" mocked
Sergeant Stinkbug. "Did you draw
them with crayons, too?"

"No," said Lucy. "They're *real* . . .

. . . and they're right behind you!"
Sergeant Stinkbug turned and
saw Fudgie, Cupcake, and Waffles.
"Help!" he screamed. The
Automatic Snatcher Arm let go of
Lucy and she fell . . .

. . . right into the Mighty Robot's hand.
"Nice catch!" said Lucy.

Ricky's Mighty Robot grabbed
Sergeant Stinkbug's Attack Pod
and held it tightly.

"All right," said Ricky, "what's
going on here?"

"*Ooh*, nothing," said Sergeant
Stinkbug, as he reached down
and pushed the EMERGENCY
ATTACK button on his wrist.

Suddenly, the Giant Spaceship floating above Earth opened up. Two Warrior Stinkbugs flew out of the spaceship and down to Sergeant Stinkbug's side. They were ready to attack.

CHAPTER SEVEN
THE BIG FIGHT

Sergeant Stinkbug reached into his belt and grabbed two round gumballs.

"My Grow-Big Gumballs should do the trick," laughed the evil Sergeant. "Here you go, my uglies!"

He threw the gumballs into the Warrior Stinkbugs' mouths.

The Warriors chewed and chewed, and they grew bigger and bigger and bigger. Then they attacked Ricky's Robot.

The Stupid Stinkbugs started
their assault with a super-smashin'
swinger stomp.

But Ricky's Robot bounced back
with a bone-bustin' blast from his
bionic breastplate.

Then he finished his fight for
freedom with a free-flyin' foot
in their funky faces.

CHAPTER EIGHT
CAPTURED

Ricky's Mighty Robot was victorious, but not for long. Sergeant Stinkbug leaned out of his Attack Pod and tossed more Grow-Big Gumballs into the mouths of his Warrior Stinkbugs.

As the Warriors chewed, they
grew and grew and grew some more.

Soon the Warriors were ten times
bigger than Ricky's Mighty Robot.

One of them grabbed Ricky's Robot
in its gigantic fist and prepared to
pound him to pieces.

"We've got to save my Robot!" cried Ricky.

Together, Ricky, Lucy, and Waffles worked out a plan.

Fudgie and Cupcake wanted to help, too, but they couldn't fly.

"You boys just stay here and think good thoughts!" said Lucy. "We'll be back soon, and everything will be fine!"

Ricky, Lucy, and Waffles flew up
to Sergeant Stinkbug's Attack Pod.

"Let go of my Robot right now,"
yelled Ricky, "or you'll be sorry!"

"You're the one who's going to be
sorry," laughed Sergeant Stinkbug. He
pressed a button on his ship and sprayed
our three heroes with Super-Stenchy
Stink-Gas.

The Automatic Snatcher Arm reached out, grabbed Ricky, Lucy, and Waffles, and held them tightly. Then Sergeant Stinkbug called for his troops.

The Giant Spaceship opened up.
Suddenly, hundreds of Attack Pods
poured out, lining up in formation.

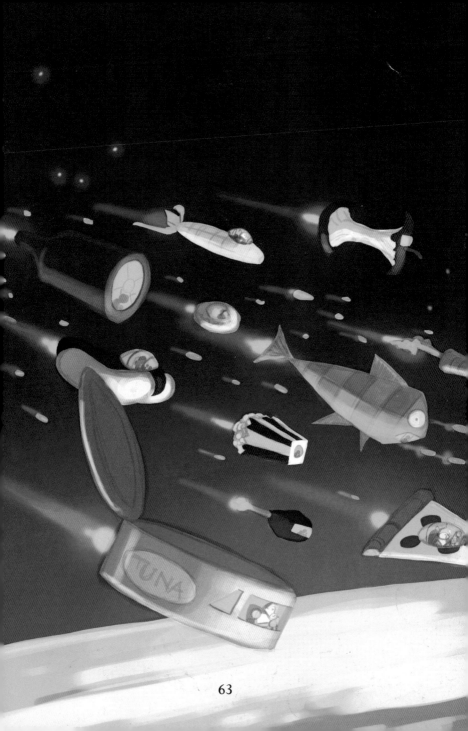

CHAPTER NINE
FUDGIE AND CUPCAKE TO THE RESCUE

Fudgie and Cupcake watched the horror unfold above their heads. It looked like the end of the world. They knew they couldn't fly, but they still had to do *something*.

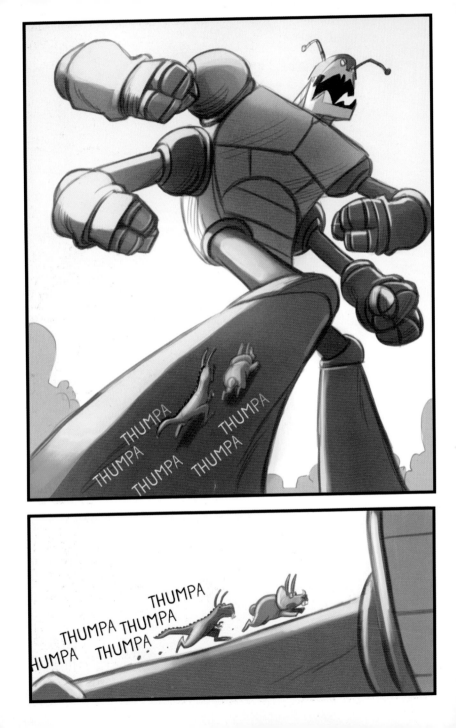

Fudgie rummaged through the Attack Pod until he found the Grow-Big Gumballs.

"Good boy, Fudgie!" said Ricky.

Fudgie wagged his fluffy tail
and tossed the bag of gumballs
into Ricky's hands. Ricky popped
six gumballs into his mouth, then
chewed and chewed . . .

. . . and grew and grew and grew!

Now Ricky was as big as the Warrior Stinkbugs. He grabbed his Mighty Robot out of their hands and tucked him into his shirt pocket.

"Don't worry, Mighty Robot," said Ricky, "it's *my* turn to save the day!"

CHAPTER TEN
THE BIG BATTLE
(IN FLIP-O-RAMA™)

FLIP-O
HEY, KIDS! YOU CAN ANIMATE THE ACTION BY FOLLOWING THESE EASY STEPS!

-RAMA
HERE'S HOW IT WORKS!

STEP 1
Place your *left* hand inside the dotted lines marked "LEFT HAND HERE." Hold the book open *flat*.

STEP 2
Grasp the *right-hand* page with your right thumb and index finger (inside the dotted lines marked "RIGHT THUMB HERE").

STEP 3
Now *quickly* flip the right-hand page back and forth until the picture appears to be *animated*.

(For extra fun, try adding your own sound-effects!)

FLIP-O-RAMA 1

(pages 79 and 81)

Remember, flip *only* page 79.
While you are flipping, be sure you
can see the picture on page 79
and the one on page 81.
If you flip quickly, the two
pictures will start to look like
<u>one</u> *animated* picture.

Don't forget to add
your own sound-effects!

LEFT HAND HERE

THE STUPID STINKBUGS ATTACKED.

RIGHT
THUMB
HERE

RIGHT
INDEX
FINGER
HERE

80

THE STUPID
STINKBUGS ATTACKED.

FLIP-O-RAMA 2

(pages 83 and 85)

Remember, flip *only* page 83.
While you are flipping, be sure you
can see the picture on page 83
and the one on page 85.
If you flip quickly, the two
pictures will start to look like
<u>one</u> *animated* picture.

Don't forget to add
your own sound-effects!

LEFT HAND HERE

RICKY FOUGHT BACK.

RIGHT
THUMB
HERE

RIGHT
INDEX
FINGER
HERE

84

RICKY FOUGHT BACK.

FLIP-O-RAMA 3

(pages 87 and 89)

Remember, flip *only* page 87.
While you are flipping, be sure you
can see the picture on page 87
and the one on page 89.
If you flip quickly, the two
pictures will start to look like
<u>one</u> *animated* picture.

Don't forget to add
your own sound-effects!

LEFT HAND HERE

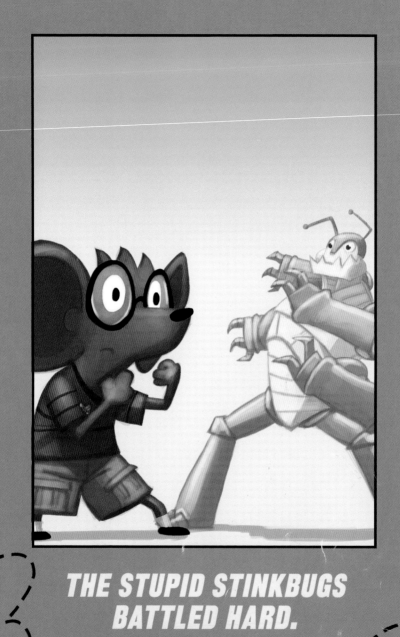

THE STUPID STINKBUGS BATTLED HARD.

RIGHT
THUMB
HERE

88

THE STUPID STINKBUGS
BATTLED HARD.

FLIP-O-RAMA 4

(pages 91 and 93)

Remember, flip *only* page 91.
While you are flipping, be sure you
can see the picture on page 91
and the one on page 93.
If you flip quickly, the two
pictures will start to look like
<u>one</u> *animated* picture.

Don't forget to add
your own sound-effects!

LEFT HAND HERE

RICKY BATTLED HARDER.

RICKY BATTLED HARDER.

FLIP-O-RAMA 5

(pages 95 and 97)

Remember, flip *only* page 95.
While you are flipping, be sure you
can see the picture on page 95
and the one on page 97.
If you flip quickly, the two
pictures will start to look like
<u>one</u> *animated* picture.

Don't forget to add
your own sound-effects!

LEFT HAND HERE

RICKY RICOTTA
WON THE WAR.

RIGHT
THUMB
HERE

RIGHT
INDEX
FINGER
HERE

RICKY RICOTTA
WON THE WAR.

CHAPTER ELEVEN
THE FINAL ATTACK

Ricky had won his battle with the giant Warrior Stinkbugs.

But Sergeant Stinkbug still had one more trick up his sleeve. He pressed a button on his wrist and called for his Attack Pod Troops to invade.

Suddenly, hundreds of Attack Pods started zooming toward Earth.

"Oh, NO!" cried Ricky. "They're EVERYWHERE!"

I'VE GOTTA GET TO HIGHER GROUND!

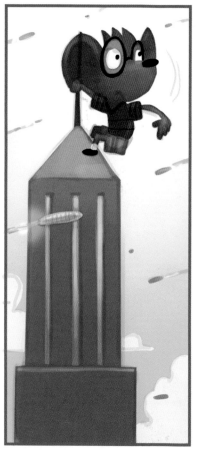

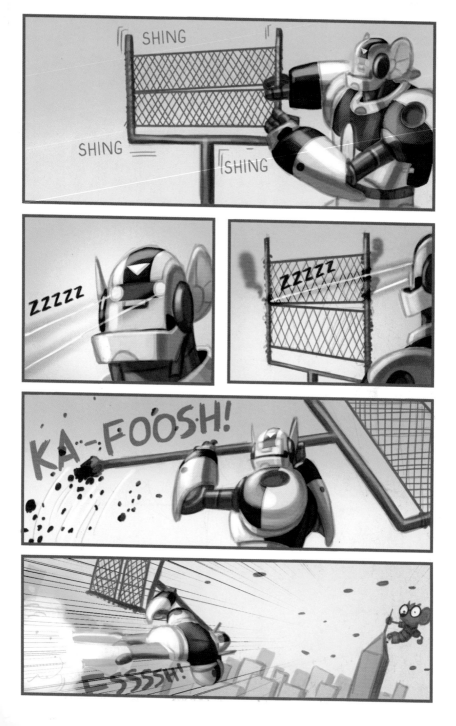

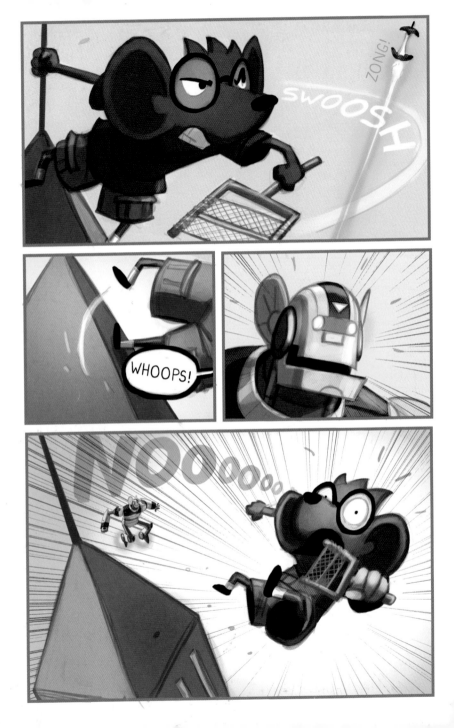

Suddenly, a giant hand emerged from a cloud and caught Ricky.

It was Lucy. She had chewed up the rest of the bag of gumballs when nobody was looking.

"I couldn't help it," said Lucy. "I just *love* gumballs!"

Lucy reached into outer space and opened up the Giant Spaceship. With it, she scooped up all of the tiny Attack Pods. Then she shoved the two Warrior Stinkbugs inside and slammed the lid closed.

With one mighty throw, Lucy tossed the mangled spaceship all the way back to Saturn.

"Well," said Lucy, "that takes care of that!"

CHAPTER TWELVE
JUST DESSERTS

Fudgie and Waffles had found a bag of Super-Shrinking Saltwater Taffy inside Sergeant Stinkbug's Attack Pod.

They gave the bag to Ricky's Robot, and he fed it to Ricky and Lucy.

Soon, the two cousins had
shrunk back to their normal sizes.
Together, the six friends
flew Sergeant Stinkbug to the
Squeakyville jail.

Then they zoomed back to
Lucy's house just in time for dessert.
The grown-ups brought out
chocolate-chip cheesecake for
everybody.

"We heard loud noises out here," said Auntie Ethel.

"What have you kids been up to?" asked Uncle Freddie.

"Well, a bad guy tried to steal my rubies," said Lucy, "but Ricky's Robot beat up the Stinkbugs. Then Fudgie found some gumballs and I grew big and clobbered the Attack Pods and . . ."

"Boy," said Ricky's mother, "those kids sure have vivid imaginations!"

"I know that Lucy gets on your nerves sometimes," Ricky's dad whispered, "but thank you for being nice to her anyway."

"No problem," said Ricky . . .

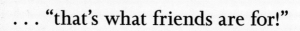

... "that's what friends are for!"

READY FOR

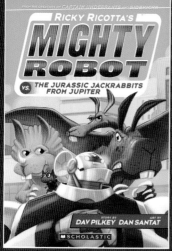

FROM THE CREATORS OF CAPTAIN UNDERPANTS AND SIDEKICKS

RICKY RICOTTA'S

MIGHTY ROBOT

VS. THE JURASSIC JACKRABBITS FROM JUPITER

STORY BY DAV PILKEY ART BY DAN SANTAT

SCHOLASTIC

FROM THE CREATORS OF CAPTAIN UNDERPANTS AND SIDEKICKS

RICKY RICOTTA'S

MIGHTY ROBOT

VS. THE STUPID STINKBUGS FROM SATURN

STORY BY DAV PILKEY ART BY DAN SANTAT

SCHOLASTIC

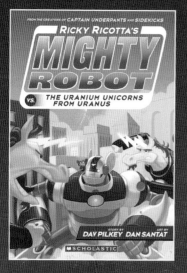

FROM THE CREATORS OF CAPTAIN UNDERPANTS AND SIDEKICKS

RICKY RICOTTA'S

MIGHTY ROBOT

VS. THE URANIUM UNICORNS FROM URANUS

STORY BY DAV PILKEY ART BY DAN SANTAT

SCHOLASTIC

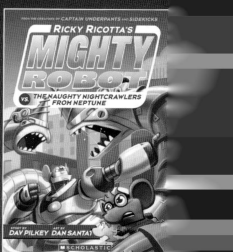

FROM THE CREATORS OF CAPTAIN UNDERPANTS AND SIDEKICKS

RICKY RICOTTA'S

MIGHTY ROBOT

VS. THE NAUGHTY NIGHTCRAWLERS FROM NEPTUNE

STORY BY DAV PILKEY ART BY DAN SANTAT

SCHOLASTIC

DAV PILKEY

has written and illustrated more than fifty books for children, including *The Paperboy*, a Caldecott Honor book; *Dog Breath: The Horrible Trouble with Hally Tosis*, winner of the California Young Reader Medal; and the IRA Children's Choice Dumb Bunnies series. He is also the creator of the *New York Times* best-selling Captain Underpants books. Dav lives in the Pacific Northwest with his wife. Find him online at www.pilkey.com.

DAN SANTAT

is the writer and illustrator of the picture book *The Adventures of Beekle: The Unimaginary Friend*. He is also the creator of the graphic novel *Sidekicks* and has illustrated many acclaimed picture books, including the *New York Times* bestseller *Because I'm Your Dad* by Ahmet Zappa and *Crankenstein* by Samantha Berger. Dan also created the Disney animated hit *The Replacements*. He lives in Southern California with his family. Find him online at www.dantat.com.